9780967772905
AF574951

Written by Ron Swisher **Illustrated by Gary Swisher**

A father and son production

This book was inspired by the men and women of the United States Postal Service. Their dedication and determination to deliver every letter and parcel with the same level of care and concern should inspire us all

The text is Bookman Old style

Ron Swisher, TRB Publishing
P. O. Box 68
Yoder, WY. 82244-0068
Printed and bound in the UNITED STATES OF AMERICA

I'm just an ordinary letter. Much like one that you might send
to your grandma, your grandpa, or to a pen pal friend.

When you stick a stamp on my chest and drop me in the mail,
I may go in an airplane, or on a mule down a canyon trail.

Dan and Bill wrote a message to Jay and Wendy far away.
It said, “We want to come see you. Is there a place for us to stay?”

They put me in a mailbox, where I lean against the side.
Then the letter carrier picks me up and gives me quite a ride.

I'm in a small white truck, thinking, "Hey, this is really cool!"
I travel to the post office. The one just past the school.

As I'm waiting on the loading dock I see an eagle on a big white truck.
It takes me to a bigger place, and Wow! am I in luck!

On belts, over wheels, and rollers, I have some really great rides,
around, over, and under, I laugh 'til I hurt my sides!

I know what my message says and with friends I start to chat.
Some keep their messages secret, like Ms. Diamond Trim, the "Flat."

Her message is quite personal and very carefully concealed.
To only her addressee can her message be revealed.

She's larger than I am, but she isn't any older.
She's really big enough to hold a large manila folder.

A chunky is a small package, but he was coming apart.
So postal folks taped him up to save his supplies of art.

I see a little letter with a blank look on his face.
He's crying, "I'm just 'Nixie,' a letter without a good
address to take me anyplace."

A woman comes and picks him up. I hear her as she says,
"You're not lost forever, we'll fix you, so you won't be such a mess."

"The one who addressed you was careless that's for sure,
we'll correct your address and that will be your cure."

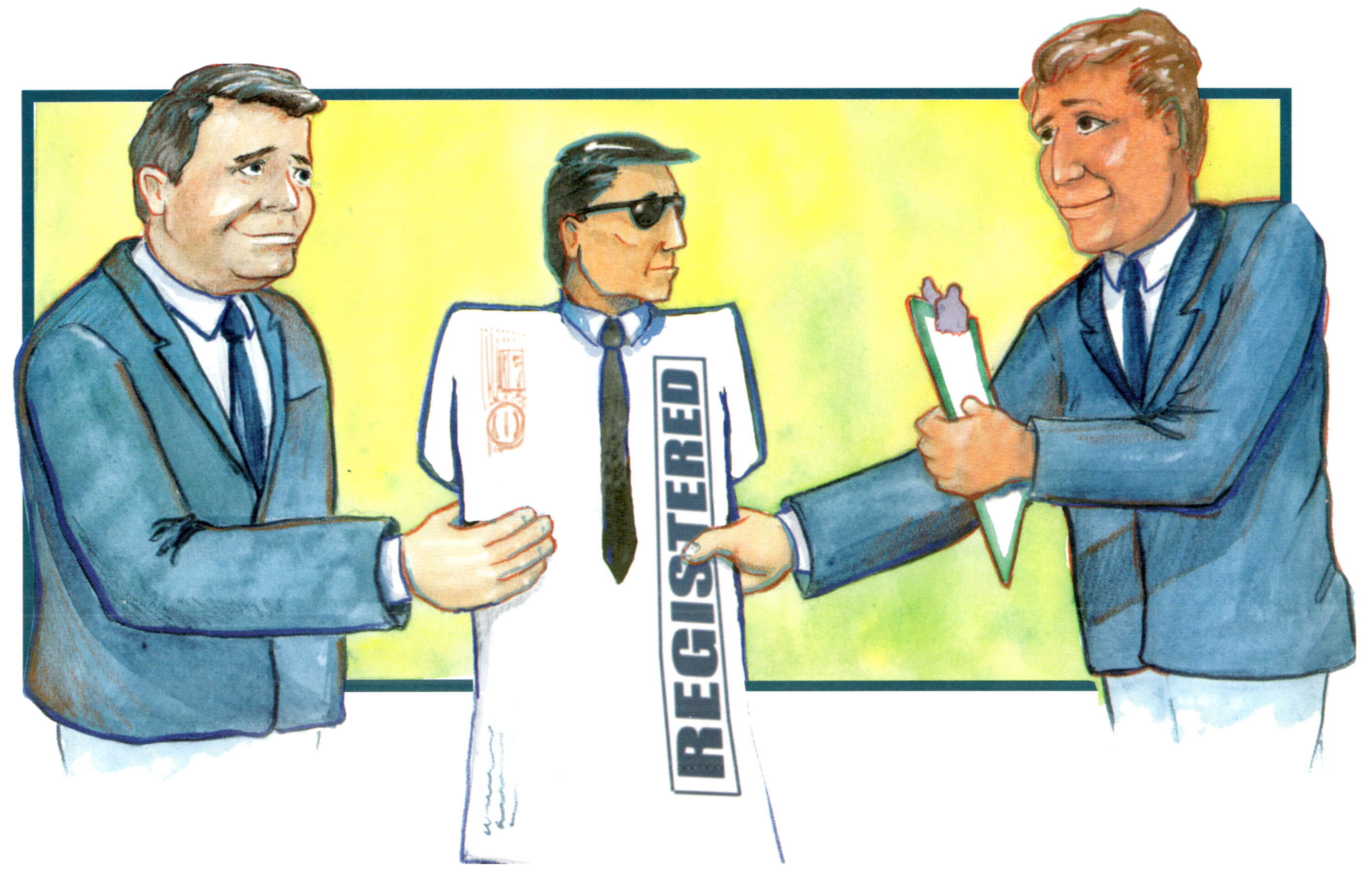

Reggie Registered must really be the most valued in the land.
Someone has to sign for him, each time he changes hands.

He has stamps all over him, but nobody can look inside.
I hear he holds a diamond ring, for a groom to give his bride.

Maggie Magazine hasn't said much, as she sits on a stack by the wall.
She says, "I'll wait 'til I'm delivered, then I'll get to 'tell all."

The sun has not yet risen as we're loaded to "hit the road."
Chunky, Nixie, and all the gang are shuffled in the load.

Suddenly I hear a peeping sound. I wonder what it is.
As best I can, I look around to see what I have missed.

Then I spot it! A large box addressed to Truxton on Route 66.
And can you guess what's peeping...?

Its full of baby chicks!!!

They aren't going as far as we will, but they are lots of fun to see.
One hundred baby chicks, traveling in the mail like me.

At the Peach Springs Post Office we get a breath of fresh air.
Then we see a “walk-in” freezer with large boxes everywhere.

Some parcels full of frozen food are “cooling it” in there.
Like Henry Hot Dog, Sloppy Joe, and my friend, French Fry Pierre.

Cowboy Bud, in a pickup truck, takes us on another ride
to the edge of a large red canyon, and we can barely see the other side.

Twenty mules are waiting to take us on our way.
Each mule has a name, I learned some of them today.

I'm assigned to Rabbit. With those long ears, his name seems right.
Chunky will ride Snowball,
a short mule who is pure white.

Bud sorts all of the parcels and then checks each mule's old shoes.
Rabbit needs some new shoes, and Snowball's shoes are loose.

The kids will all be waiting,
to see what comes down
the trail.

Everything they eat and wear
must get to them by mail.

We see some black clouds gathering above the canyon rim.
But Brian is our wrangler, and we put our trust in him.

Just two miles down an eight mile trail, it begins to rain real hard.
I can tell by Brian's worried face, it catches him off guard.

Rain water running off the cliffs, causes many waterfalls.
Some are wide and powerful, some a thousand feet tall.

Water running down the canyon is washing the trail away.
Every ravine becomes a river. Will we get safely down today?

We are well protected from rainfall coming down.
Then Snowball slips and falls. I'm afraid that he will drown.

Snowball can swim and swim he does, right down the rushing stream.
Until he gets his footing back, it seems like a bad dream.

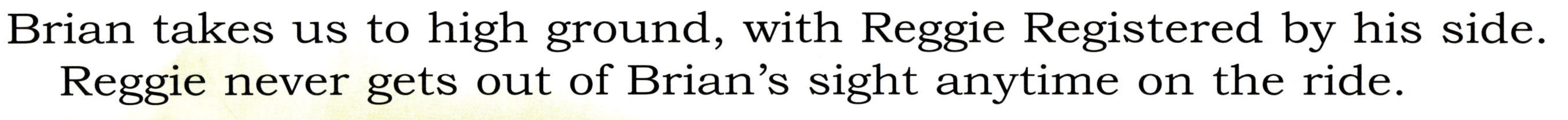

Brian takes us to high ground, with Reggie Registered by his side.
Reggie never gets out of Brian's sight anytime on the ride.

Poor Henry Hot Dog and Sloppy Joe are getting pretty wet.
These two guys and French Fry Pierre started frozen, don't forget.

Ms. Diamond Trim and Maggie still haven't said a word.
They're waiting to tell their addressee everything they've heard.

Remember when poor Nixie thought that he was "lost" that day?
Nixie now thinks this is worse, so here's what I say.

"Don't worry, we'll get there. We're in Postal Service hands.
THE MAIL MUST GO THROUGH, it's true, and its a legend of our land!"

It stops raining and, very quickly, there is no stream at all.
Now there's only dripping rocks where there had been a waterfall.

A couple of hours later, we come to another stream,
but this one's not flooded. The water is "blue-green."

We let the mules all get a drink and it's getting kind of hot.
Up ahead we see some houses and lots of children running about.

There is one entire family. Mother, Father, Son, and Daughter.
In their native language, Havasupai means "People of the Blue-Green Water."

The mules stop at the post office. The people gather 'round.
They unload the mail and then they sort it on the ground.

The letters are quickly taken in. The books go to the school.
French Fry Pierre and his gang, go to the Cafe to keep their "cool."

Jay and Wendy have a post office box. That's where I thought I'd stay, but they are waiting for me, so I'm handed to them today.

Everybody likes to get letters. I gave Jay and Wendy a special thrill.
They open my flap and read my message from their good friends, Dan and Bill.

They put me down to tell their mom and then read my message again.
I'm sure my message was shared with dozens of their friends.

Even though I am delivered, the joy I bring will last.
If you think it's fun getting a letter, try being one.....**IT'S A BLAST!!!**

Our Mail system goes from the sophisticated machinery found in highly automated post offices in large metropolitan areas, to the simplicity of a pack mule with ropes and straps in the Havasu Canyon. Whatever the location, the men and women of the United States Postal Service are on the job because **"The Mail Must Go Through!"**

The Havasu Canyon is part of the Grand Canyon and, thus, requires special care to preserve its natural beauty. The U.S. Postal Service honors this with its unique mail delivery...pack mules. Everything you can imagine is delivered through the mail due to its timeliness and dependability...the Postal Service has very little competition in the Havasu Canyon.

GLOSSARY OF TERMS AND FACTS

DIAMOND TRIM FLAT: A "flat" is a large piece of mail. A "Diamond Trim Flat" is First Class mail with green diamond-shaped patterns on all four edges. This makes it easier to see when it is in a bundle of "flat" mail.

CHUNKY: A parcel too large to fit in a bundle of "flats," but not as large as the larger packages.

SUPAI: A village of approximately 350 Indians of the Havasupai Tribe located in Havasu Canyon, a remote portion of the greater Grand Canyon of Arizona.

NIXIE: A letter without proper address, but one that usually can be corrected by a knowledgeable Postal employee.

REGISTERED MAIL: Letters or parcels that are very valuable. They may be insured for large amounts of money. The Hope Diamond was sent by Registered Mail to the Smithsonian Museum in Washington, D.C. It must be signed for by EACH person who handles it.

BABY CHICKS IN THE MAIL: Thousands of baby chicks, ducks, turkeys, quail, geese, and other baby fowl are mailed each year.

WALK-IN FREEZER IN A POST OFFICE: This is unusual, but true at Peach Springs, AZ. The people of Supai receive most of their groceries by mail. The frozen food is kept in the freezer until taken to the edge of the Canyon and loaded on the mules.

MULE: A mule's mother is a mare (horse) and it's father is a mule or donkey. It is rare for a female mule to give birth to a foal.

MULE SHOES: Mule shoes do not look like yours or mine. Like horse shoes, they are made of metal to protect the animal's hooves from the rocks on the rugged canyon trails.

HAVASUPAI, People Of The Blue-Green Water: Water of the streams and waterfalls is a beautiful blue-green color. It is from an underground river that was exposed when the canyon carved deep into the Earth. The Indians got their name from this water.

LETTERS AS KEEPSAKES: Telephone, fax, and e-mail are wonderful forms of communication, but letters are forever. Many people save special letters for a lifetime. MAIL A LETTER TODAY TO SOMEONE YOU LOVE. IT WILL MAKE THEM VERY HAPPY.

This book is based on the true story of mail delivery to Supai five days a week all year.
It is a testimony to the many dedicated employees of the UNITED STATES POSTAL SERVICE who sort, transport, and deliver the mail everywhere, every day.

If you enjoyed this "Canyon Adventure"
WATCH FOR FUTURE ADVENTURES IN THE SERIES...

"THE MAIL MUST GO THROUGH"

Let the mail take you on adventures to:

AN AMISH FARM IN THE HEARTLAND OF AMERICA

AN ESKIMO VILLAGE IN ALASKA

THE INNER CITY OF A LARGE METROPOLIS

A COMMUNITY WHERE MAIL COMES BY BOAT

AND MANY MORE...

For more information on these and other books in the series, send inqueries to:
TRB PUBLISHING P.O. BOX 68 YODER, WYOMING 82244-0068
Or contact the author, Ron Swisher at his studio:
P.O. BOX 679 HONAUNAU, HAWAII 96726-0679

This book is dedicated to the memory of *"Cowboy Bud"* Delaney who died in a tragic vehicle accident while delivering mail to be loaded onto the mules in Havasupai Canyon on January 27, 1999, and to his widow, Carol Delaney, who continues to see that THE MAIL MUST GO THROUGH.